SILHOUETTE

A Pair of Stories by a Student

By Enze Zhang

Illustrated by Yifan Chen

Paperback ISBN: 979-8-9883619-4-7
Ebook ISBN: 979-8-9883619-5-4
Library of Congress Control Number: 2025944649

for information, or to contact the publisher: eric@ericwiberg.com
design and layout by Abdul Rehman Qureshi: writingpanacea@gmail.com

First Edition. Printed in the United States of America

Island Books

To my family, especially my grandmother,

To my teachers, Mr. Eric Wiberg and Mr. Johnny Zhong,

Thank you for all the inspiration, support, and guidance that made this book possible.

CONTENTS:

STANLEE

Our school's gate was wildly different from the one's other schools around Pomona had. It was one of those intimidating gates you see at old-fashioned orphanages or asylums. The two tall stone pillars with a stupid gargoyle each on top were connected by webs of rusty iron bars. I wonder why they designed a school gate like this. They've probably copied the blueprint of a haunted house at a cheap carnival. I'm more inclined to think that this stupid school, which is called Backers, sent some men who are jacked as hell to go steal this gate and then plant it back at school. I can imagine twenty mercenaries with one hundred and sixty abs in total pulling the gates up from the ground the way trees are pulled up from the roots. Poor gates.

And a few months ago, right before spring break, when I saw my grandma standing in front of the gate like a god dam stump, I wanted to hang myself. I was supposed to go back to New York with my mom and dad. They would probably take me to a Broadway show, to our favorite

Italian restaurant and to all that good stuff.

They called me last night, literally twenty hours before the flight, and told me that the plane was cancelled.

"Oh, I'm so sorry, honey, the airline company said due to bad weather conditions they had to delay your flight to three weeks later!" mom said it in her usual sweet tone.

"Your dad has been negotiating with the airline company, he was working very hard," she said as she put her phone next to dad. He was arguing with the poor airline company workers.

He yelled at the line receiver: "You better give me a valid reason! I'm going to show you who's the real boss!" Then I heard him slam his phone onto the table. You got to see how my stepdad plays tough by being angry when he faces any difficulties. My mom loved it somehow.

"Darling, we called your grandma, you can live with her for the following two week and enjoy some great family bonding time, isn't that sweet!" mom squeaked. Her voice was so syrupy that I thought it was marinated with honey and then soaked in a mixture of ten different jams and marmalades.

"Sure, fine, don't worry," I replied, then I just left my phone on my table to lie there lifelessly.

That night, I tried not to think of how mom and stepdad probably spent their night enjoying romantic dinner at our favorite Italian restaurant or smooching in a Broadway theater. Instead, I attempted to recall anything useful about grandma. She was five foot tall, never wore a dress   (at least that is what she told me)   and always had a weird brownish flat cap on. Her name is Stanlee, which is not a name you would relate to an "old kind grandma". She is not one of those types of grandparents because she spoke and acted like a cowboy and a bounty hunter from the Wild West. Not the mediocre ones. She was the nasty ones.

The last time we met was at a family reunion ten years ago when I was six. I was being a stupid little prick by pushing one of my younger cousins to the floor and robbing her chocolate bar. That made my grandma angry. I remember how this mad lady chased me with her right foot slipper in her hand. She was swinging it as if she was King Arthur holding the Excalibur that she freshly pulled out of the stone. Have you ever heard of how in prehistoric times, some Africans hunt? After spotting their prey, they start jogging after it, at a constant pace. The animal, usually an antelope or similar, sees a bunch of people coming after it, so it dashes out of the hunters' sight.

The poor animal sprints for a long time, and it decides to take a break, but just when it thinks it has escaped, the hunters have already caught up with it. So, the animal runs for its life again, decides to take a rest after being at what it thinks is a safe distance, only to then realize that the hunters caught up again!

This treacherous cycle continues until the antelope faints due to extreme tiredness. Thats basically what happened that day; I was the poor antelope, and my grandma was a top-notch hunter. While I could imagine her skinning me and peeling of the meat from my bones the way the African hunters handled their dead prey, she didn't do it. Instead, her spanking of me with her slippers and my desperate howling formed a brutal yet harmonious symphony. I really don't want to spend this lovely two-week spring break with this lady who could strangle me like a KGB agent.

Since the principal decided to spend the entire morning in the lecture hall giving long wordy speeches about being grateful and all that nonsense, we only had one class in the afternoon before the break. Our teacher already went on vacation, so they got a poor guy to sub in for our class. No one wanted to teach nor learn under the March sunlight reflected through the window, so the teacher put on "Ferris Bueller's Day Off" and laid back on his chair. I looked out of the window as the Ferris rode the red Firari. There was a boy who looked like a god damn spaghetti meatball messing around on his red bike. He's even got a small bike helmet on.

Later that afternoon, I carried my big green suitcase and walked to the gates. I heard a loud "plush" noise and felt something warm landing on my shoulder. I lifted my head and saw two crows flying past me. Love that bird crap. Its color matches my outfit beautifully.

As I was filling out my break pass at the security, I saw classmates and even strangers waving goodbye to their friends. That stupid boy over there, the one who looked like a meatball with an orange wig, bragged for two months about how his parents were going to take him to the Ritz Hotel.

"My father has an Ultimate VIP card to the Ritz hotel, and he will take me there. I could bring you some souvenirs!" He squeaked when I saw him through the window.

"Great! Wonderful! Good for you!" I replied, but obviously, he wasn't listening.

"VIP - more like Viciously Ignorant Pigling," I whispered to myself.

The spaghetti meatball hopped onto his red bike and biked around the gate.

"*Clark, Crack, Ringaling, Crack.*" The sound of a metal behemoth roaring and stomping its way towards the gothic-style school gate made me look that way. It was a very sad-looking mini truck. The rusting of its metal covering and the mixture of sand with dirt was like a scourge that spread and consumed a lot of its originally white body. If the tires can speak, they'd be going a strike for shorter work time and better working conditions.

It stopped, and a short lady with a brown flat cap hopped out of the mini truck, shut the door with a goddamn fierce back kick, and then stomped her way towards me. Oh boy. It's Grandma Stanlee.

"Hey Kiddo! Haven't seen you in a very long time!" She yelled at me while she walked

towards me, totally ignoring about twenty other students and their parents staring at her.

Have you ever seen those reflex balls boxers hit over and over, and how they bounce forwards and backwards ridiculously when hit? Well, my grandma whacked my head like one of those sandbags, and it made her crack up a little bit.

"Ha! You gotta strengthen your neck! That's the way we say hello to you weak and feeble young people! Haha!" She laughed while patting my shoulders.

"Stanlee, it hurts! And now everyone is looking!" I whispered. "Anyways please wait for me in the truck, I'll need to fill in this pass request quickly."

"Ha!! Don't be a sissy, Kiddo! I'll wait for ya next to the truck! I wanna stand for a lil' bit," she laughed.

"Hey kiddo, are you done? Get in the car," Stanlee commanded. It's only been like one minute.

I hurried through the paperwork, left it on the security table, and then slammed the door shut.

"Don't slam the door! What's the matter with you?" the weird and grumpy old lady asked. She then started the engine of the car, or should I say the engine of an artifact.

"Sorry," I tried to answer using the bare minimum of words. The road conditions are terrible. The cracks that are all over the roads are connected to each other. If you found a modern artist and gave him a bird-eye view of our roads, they would have believed that you were showing him a masterpiece of surrealist art. On a rainy day, rain drops accumulated inside the cracks, and they flood the roads.   These road crevices are almost like canals.

"Hey! Check the paper bag in the back seat!" Stanlee commanded light-heartedly. There were two pieces of dry brownies with the same crack as the ones on the poor roads.

"I heard that you liked a sweet treat or two, so I got them for us, ha!" She laughed and said as she reached her hands from the steering wheel into the bag.

"Oh! Thanks-"

"Just take one! I'll beat you with my slippers just like ten years ago at the family reunion if you take my piece! Ha!" She quickly grabbed one piece with her palm and shoved it into her mouth in one bite, leaving brown crumbs behind. The dried-up brownies were sort of stale and crumbly, and I stared with doubt at them, wondering whether they should end up in my stomach or not.

"Come on Kiddo don't be a puss! If an old grandma is eating it just fine, you'll be fine! IIa!" She talked as if she was a gangster boss giving a speech to me, the new member, an inspiring rally before we rob a bank or something.

"How's school been? You are doing well, right?' She spoke again after swallowing it.

"Great." I wasn't paying attention. I found a bag of chips under the seat, and somehow, I started reading its nutrition chart.

"Kiddo, are you listening at all even?" She saw me through the rear-view mirror. I didn't respond.

"60% of daily recognized fat value, that's a lot of calories," I muttered.

"You boys have no respect at all!" She started her long rant in a joking tone. I was still a speech, though. I wasn't a huge fan of listening to an old lady giving her speeches, so I looked outside of my window. We were on the highway, and there was a dreadful traffic jam. Each car was moving at the shocking speed of one millimeter per minute. I looked up into the sky because there wasn't anything better to look at. There were two seagulls, a large one and a younger one. They flew above the cars, passed the highway, and into the clouds.

My stereotype of seagulls is that they are stupid birds which steal bread from stupid people taking a sunbath on the beach. I've never seen seagulls who flew so freely. It somehow depressed me a little. I wonder why I can't feel anything cool. I got a badass grandma who got me brownies, which are my favorite desserts. I get to know her for a couple of weeks, and I don't desperately want to be the third wheel when my mom and stepdad are French kissing. Still, I felt the two stupid seagulls were having a better time than me.

I had to escape.

"All right Kiddo, we're here," my grandma said as she parked the car and walked towards the door.

Her house was rather interesting. She was living in this small cottage that randomly appeared in a normal neighborhood. It looked like an overbaked breakfast bun. She painted the walls with a mixture of dreadful brownish color and the grayish black color of coal.

I asked: "Why did you paint your house like this?" -I was curious. There must be some reason behind such peculiar artistic choices.

"I like the color, and it's none of your business. My taste is indisputable," she refuted. "Now get inside the room and make yourself comfortable, 'cause I don't have all the time to do it.

I sighed, then dragged my oil-green suitcase into the room.

"Ha! Kiddo, you were mocking my taste, and yet now, look at your suitcase, what can I say! Ha!" Stanlee laughed.

"*Whack*," she slapped my head and commanded satirically,"Hurry up and get your butt into the room, will ya?"

There isn't much in the living room. A wine-red couch, an enormous 18inch TV, a table with one of its legs taped onto its body, some poor miserable chairs that have obviously been through serious catastrophes, and a kitchen that smells like one of those very dirty restaurants which serves you dead rat in your tomato soup.

"There are two floors and an attic. Take your suitcase up to the attic, and after dinner, I'll go find you some bedsheets and blankets." she yelled while she walked into the kitchen.

The bed is cool, and I like that Persian carpet lying on the floor, but the best part of the attic is the skylight. We got back around six P.M., and the tiny skylight was like a fishing net, capturing all the red, orange, pink, or purple sunset lights swimming between the clouds. Then, it blended some reflected rainbow into the captured light, allowing the mixture to simmer, bubble, and boil. It then generously shared the colorful soup with me, pouring all of it gently and carefully through the net's opening onto the white bed. I haven't seen something this bright in a while.

Red. My father had this red leather jacket. He told me he watched Michael Jackson's music video for "Thriller" all the time when he was a kid, and he badly wanted the cool red jacket Michael wore. He couldn't afford it until he was in college, where he fried McDonald burger patties for a long time to buy a similar red jacket at a thrift store.

Orange. He peeled oranges as if he was plowing the sun, and he usually gave one for me, one for my mom, and the smallest one for himself. He told me to do the "lion face" if it's too sweet, do the "lemon face" if it's too sour, or hug him and mom if it's just right. When I hugged him, his t-shirt smelled sour, bitter, yet very sweet.

Pink. He once showed me a picture of him and mom when they were seniors in high school. He wore a pink suit with a golden tie, and she wore a dark blue slip dress. He joked about how they rented these clothes from a shop, and that the only suit left that fit his size was that pink suit. He smiled and put it on.

Purple. Every Friday afternoon my dad went to a big store to buy meat for weekend barbecues, missing ingredients for my mom's lemon pies, or some wine for them to enjoy when I was asleep. Mom puts dad on speaker when he called, and I could hear their conversations clearly. Dad always wanted to bring something along for her, and she always asked for some purple roses. I would dash to the door when I heard the doorbell ringing, seeing him grabbing bags of groceries in one hand and holding a bouquet of bright purple roses with the other.

"Hey kiddo! Dinner's ready!" Stanlee suddenly yelled; her voice like shooting fire-red steel marbles out of a shotgun, scaring the lights away and tearing the net into pieces.

"Quicker-*quicker* - time for supper!" The second round of bullets blasted the clouds into a pile of bloody mashed flesh.

"What the heck are you doing up there! Get your butt down here kiddo!" The final, deafening shot blew a hole in the ceiling.

"I'm coming!" I finally replied.

Stanlee had made spicy tomato soup. It's blood-red color, bits of tomatoes floating in the soup, and even the sad-looking toast bothered me. I chucked down the burning soup, afraid to taste its flavor. Thats my dad's favorite dish, and he used to make it very often for me and my mom.

"Ha kiddo, why ya eating so fast? No one's gonna come and steal the soup from you!" Stanlee joked as she dipped the bread inside the soup and took a gigantic bit out of it, spilling some soup onto her jacket and the table. She seems oblivious to it all.

"Thanks, the soup tasted great," I said to her, then ran up into the attic, hoping that all my captured colors hadn't fully escaped from the skylight net.

"You'd better do the dishes later! You know, the head chef never does the dishes! Ha!" she yelled.

When I got back to the attic, there were no more lights in the skylight. I lay on the white bed, allowing seconds then minutes then hours to pass. I feel the need to escape Stanlee, to go outside, and find those colors back.

"Excuse me, Stanlee, can I take a walk in the neighborhood?" I asked after dinner. The cold stale bread and the spicy tomato soup did taste all right, but I ate it too fast, which caused a stomach acid tsunami inside me. "Some fresh air might be helpful," I thought to myself.

"You did your dishes, kiddo?" She yelled from her room while watching some random soap opera. Stanlee has a talent for finding old and weird shows on her phone that the T.V. stations no longer broadcast.

"Yep," I replied. There was a long pause where the squeaking of T.V. characters filled the room.

"Sure kiddo, but you gotta be back by nine!" Stanlee called as she walked out of the room into the kitchen to check her plates and get some lemonade.

"Thanks!" I called back as I ran out the door.

I could escape right now, but if I don't come back by 9 p.m. and she gets me, the odds of leaving her house in the future are extremely slim. My plan is to get familiar with the neighborhood and maybe find a bike or two. With a bike, I could go very far and still return at the required time.

I remember that V.I.P. meatball dude left his bike at the security gates without a lock. He said he believed in the kindness and integrity of people.

"Well, I'm not going to steal it, I'm just borrowing it for a couple of weeks with low probability of returning it. He doesn't need it anyways. Not that a meatball could ride a bike or anything." I thought.

The last bit of sunset has faded from streets, headed for their own homes in the sky, leaving the streetlamps glimmering by themselves. The other source of light were small diners around the corner. One gigantic red and yellow light sign read, "Mr. Dylan's Magical Diner". Its bright, superficial colors drew me in like a moth to a flame.

There was nothing but two thick layers of silence inside the Diner. The first layer is a result of the lack of human interaction. No crying children; no awkward teens sipping on smoothies; no balding men gulping on cold, industrialized beer; no old couples chewing salad with their dentures. The second layer of silence infiltrated when I sat on the greasy purple swivel chair next to the counter. The dull lights, fading colors on numerous objects, rotten table-corners, and spider webs on the ceiling slowly consumed the cheers of happiness and celebration echoing in the halls. They attempted to reappropriate their ravenous appetite that they tried to hide but eventually failed with silence. No people. No colors - only silence.

"Yo, we're closed." A rough, oily, yet intimidating voice jumped up behind me. I turned around and saw a six-foot, bear-like man with hair covering his arms and a nasty full beard that looked like a mask. Logic told me to run as fast as I could, but suddenly I wasn't able to command them anymore.

"Sorry sir I didn't know that you were closed. I'm very sorry and..."

"Cut the crap. What do you think you're doing around here?" the gigantic man interrogated.

"Sorry sir, I was just wandering around, and I was..."

"Don't repeat that stupid 'sorry sir' nonsense! You're a pickpocket, am I right?"

"I'm not a thief, I just accidentally wandered inside your diner," I replied as I slowly walked backwards towards the door, so as not to present my back to him.

"Haven't seen you around, huh? Are you really here to get dinner? Or do you want me to give you a shiner?" he essentially roared into my ears. "How about this: you admit that you're a dirty little thief, and I'll let you go!" he added while rolling his fists and stretching his arms. I rarely use the word "intimidating" to describe someone's biceps.

"Why ain't you talking, kid? Tough luck, you shouldn't have entered my place!"

I should have just done what he told me and then gotten the hell out of this place. I shouldn't have even stepped inside in the first place, but there was something boiling inside me at such an inappropriate time. This force didn't want me to give up my missions to find colors.

"Back off! I'm not a thief! No one wants to steal something from this god and customer forsaken place anyways!" I yelled and immediately regretted it.

He put on a grave expression after hearing it, then stomped towards me, step by step.

"Shut it! Run! You thief!" he yelled as he grabbed the back of my T-shirt, opened the door, and threw me into the street.

"Thud." It hurt.

The cracks that are all over the roads are connected to each other like mini canals. I imagined that on a rainy day, the rainwater would fill up the crevices and then flood the streets. Then I can fold some paper boats and leave them in those temporary artificial lakes to go wherever they want.

I lay on the road for a while, staring into the unimaginably vast darkness, only with a couple of lonely stars like Christmas bells shimmering on a poor old wilting Christmas tree.

"I'm not stopping here," I whispered quietly to myself. I looked deeply into one of the stars, the shiniest one, as if I'm asking for its approval to continue my journey. It didn't say a thing as it looked back, just giving off an altering red and green light. It was a god damn airplane.

I pulled out my phone from my pocket to check the time: the

cracked screen showed the numbers "20:00." It is a forty-minute walk from the neighborhood to the school, and then I can bike at twice the speed I walk. Perfect.

"Go back to school, get the bike, and then ride back. Three simple steps. Let's go," I repeated it as I pulled myself up from the concrete ground.

The street view was kind of bland. A couple of tiny oak trees over here, some boring Japanese maple trees around the corner, stone-colored street walks with a fair amount of rubbish and soda cans as decorations, and annoying fast-food chains, such as In-N-Outs. Dad first took me to In-N-Out when I was six. I don't know which details I find more fascinating about the restaurant. The square dispensers burst out bubbly sodas water and caramel-colored syrup while rumbling gently, filling up those bright paper cups. The tall young boy at the counter smiled and handed the receipt to dad, where he took it with both hands. The fresh, spicy onions that soaked a little bit of lettuce water and meat juice exploded in my mouth. Dad took enormous bites of burgers, and he laughed with pieces of lettuce or bits of meat patties stuck onto his teeth when I looked up, and then we'd both laugh the crap out of ourselves.

I slowly wandered, fondly remembering those onions, that kind counter boy, and the bits of beef stuck onto dad's teeth in mind, back to school. The security was snoring inside his booth, and Meatball's red heavy bicycle was leaning against the wall. I tiptoed my way from a bush I was hiding in towards the bike.

"Crunch," the sound of a glass plate being shattered jolted me. The security guard was still snoring like Sleeping Beauty. I had stepped on some dried leaves.

"Caw! Caw!" a stupid crow was screeching in the treetops. It sounded like a miserable person cackling at another even more miserable person. Security was still slumbering pathetically.

I tiptoed my way to the red bike and found that it wasn't locked. I sighed with relief when I finally laid my hands on the black, leather saddle.

"Ha, sorry stupid Meatball, better get a lock next time!" I joked with myself as I hopped onto the bike.

"Warning! Warning! Warning! Warning!" The moment I quietly put my feet on the pedals, the bike started screaming like a younger sibling when an older one touched their hair.

"Hey! What are you doing!" The Sleeping Beauty woke up. His big, oily hand reached out towards the door handle as he grabbed a police baton with the other. I tried to pedal, but the bike apparently locked itself up. Now, all that's left for me to do is wait for inevitable doom.

At least the beating had a cool rhythm. After kicking and trampling me off the bike, the beating pattern was two light strokes on my waist followed by a tough stab with the relatively pointy head at my stomach. Some kicks, stepping on my fingers, and pulling me up by the collar and then slapping my face happened intermittently.

I tried to hum "We Will Rock You," alongside the beating. I might as well sing along the percussion if I'm currently the drums.

"Buddy, you're a boy, make a big noise-"

"Oh yeah! This one's definitely gonna make some real big noise!"

"Bang, whack!"

"Playing on the streets, gonna be a big man someday-"

"You dirty little thief! Street rats are going to get beaten till you'll never get to be a big man!"

"Whack, thud, plush."

"You got mud on your face, you big disgrace,"

"Whack, bam, thud."

"It's good that you know your place! I've been holding onto it for a very long time..."

"Bam, thud."

"Kicking your cans all over the place, singing-"

"Whack, bang."

The security guard yelled "And I'm going to let it all out! Thank you! For being here so I can 'legitimately' have some fun!"

"We will, we will, rock you-"

"Bang, bang, whack."

"We will, we will, rock yo

"Bang, bang, whack."

"We will, we will, rock..."

"Bang, bang, splash."

I woke up on a truck, hearing an old lady swearing in the front seat.

"That little son of a prick! Doesn't he know how to take care of himself? Oh, my goodness gracious! He is just like his God damn dad! He's even more stupid!" Stanlee's rant accompanied with the roaring of the engines and the blasting music from the Radio echoed inside the truck.

She heard me stretching my legs in the back seat, and it triggered. "Holy cow kiddo! Do you have any idea what you are doing! You almost got yourself killed! Dead! What happened was that Rock, the guy working at the diner, saw you running into his restaurant. After he threw you out,he was kinda of worried about you, wondering why the hell you were out there alone so late!   So, he followed you, and lost track of you around the school. The next minute he saw you lying on the godamn ground! If it wasn't for him, you'd be dead! D, E, A, D, DEAD! You were laying on the street, Goddamn bruises everywhere! You scared the hell out of me! Is it really that hard to trust you, to believe that you won't kill yourself accidently when you are just simply taking a walk in the goddamn neighborhood? You are getting grounded! Don't think about going anywhere else, you little..."

We did not talk when we arrived home. I instantly took off my shoes and ran up to the attic, locking the trap door behind me. It was a disastrous trip. No colors; no brilliant memories; only bruises. I could not and did not want to sleep that night because I desperately stared into the skylight, hoping to find something, anything. Any color would do, even the nasty ones. Instead, there were no colors, only darkness. I shut the skylight heavily.

I wasn't bothered by any emotions from outside. My quest for color has already planted a small, unassuming seed in the darkest corners of my being. It clenches my heart with its roots each time it draws out nutrients and colors. If I had been able to find something, or just anything during the journey, it wouldn't have been such a preoccupation. The lack of bright colors for it to indulge itself in had made the plant mad.

"Feed me!" It yelled.

"Get me those colors, feed me now!!!" It ordered.

I am physically incapable of going outside and searching for the smallest trace of colors on a very dark night, so I just allow its roots to thrash against me, leaving fresh welt like warts on flytraps until I lose consciousness.

I woke up the next day to find Stanly by the door in her pink pajamas.

"Have some fruit kid. Makes you feel better. Come get breakfast in a few minutes." she said, then turned away.

Yellow pineapples, purple grapes, pink peaches, and orange tangerines sat quietly on a Chinese porcelain plate. They were so colorful as if they grew out of the sunset and clouds. Very colorful.   So bright.

DAGGER

1

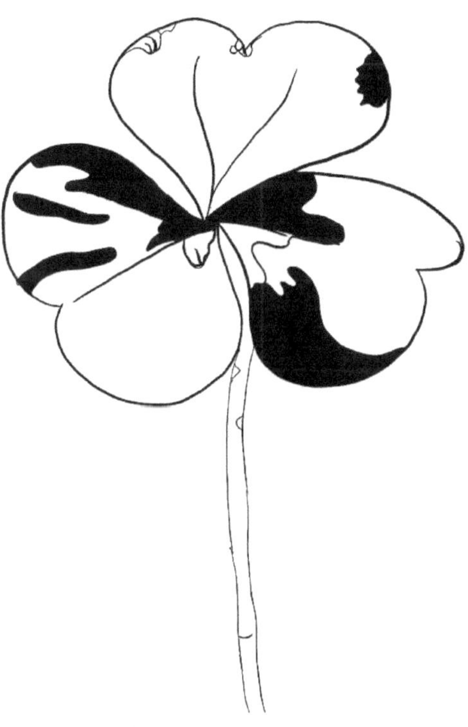

Three teenage boys sat together in the corner of their school cafeteria, having a quick lunch. Bits of east coast sunlight slid through the skylight.

"Trust me," said a boy as he stuffed the bacon sandwich into his mouth. His oval face was topped with curly and messy black hair and thick eyebrows. His dark-brown eyes weren't black holes that devoured the light in other people's eyes. No one would blame him even if he did, because humans are light-searching and stimulation-seeking creatures after all. Instead, they were mirrors that reflected all the possibilities they saw. People rarely find eyes that innocently and boldly share the colors that they see. Those eyes belonged to Josh.

"This is going to be a phenomenal adventure," he yelled happily.

"For God's sake, please don't speak with a mouthful of food," commanded another boy with light blonde hair, pointing at the crumbs Josh left on the table. The boy's shirt was buttoned from the bottom to the top. His facial features were perfectly proportioned to his diamond-square face, including the lazurite blue eyes hiding behind his glasses. Those eyes belonged to Lucas.

He whispered: "It's extremely childish and impolite, and…."

"Some seniors told me that we'll get to see some real wildlife in that forest a few miles away from our school! It is going to be magnificent!" Josh interrupted exuberantly.

"But it's dangerous out there, and we don't want to get into trouble, right?" Another boy asked in a calm but slightly trembling voice, secretly holding onto the edge of the table. The short table reached all the way to the boy's chest, and his round nose and freckles were packed onto his round face. He had black eyes, too, and if you looked carefully at his eyes, you'd realize that he must have once looked deeply into Josh's mirror eyes because he mimicked their qualities. Admiring and following people or things is natural, and he has done it very well, almost completely transforming his eyes into Josh's eyes. He is Ares.

"Please Ares - please Lucas; I promise that it will be fun!" beseeched Josh.

Lucas wiped his mouth with his napkin, folded it into a perfect square, and placed it on top of his plate as he questioned Josh: "Why you are so excited about going into a humid, rotting, nasty forest? The bears inside will gladly have you as an afternoon snack."

"Um," Josh hesitated for one second and spoke up while he took a big slurp from his juice box, "We can hide behind the trees, in that way the bears won't see us!"

"I must go with you, Josh, not because I think that it's fun. It's just that without me, both of you would likely die in the forest," said Lucas. Holding on to his grin, Josh then stared at Ares, and he received a quiet nod.

Josh yelled like a child as he dropped his bacon sandwich and hopped on to the chair like a delighted maniac.

"Huzzah! Huzzah! Our adventure now begins!"

The joy of adventure, however, was not long-lasting. He successfully attracted the attention of everyone in the entire dining hall, including the dean. Dean Tadeo marched towards our hero and dragged him from his chair by the arm.

"Hope that some detention will teach you how to behave in a public space, young man:

AFTER SCHOOL! IN MY OFFICE!" He yelled.

To the others he remonstrated:

"What are you all watching? Now EAT!!!" The dean, who looked like a grizzly bear from a distance, slammed the door as he stormed out of the dining hall.

The three boys finished lunch with the rest of the students, some terrified, some uncontrollably laughing at Josh's pure stupidity, and some just eating with their heads down. After lunch, Josh skipped to class with Lucas chasing along behind him.

"Josh! Don't skip in the hallway! It's so childish and immature! Do you know how to walk?" questioned Lucas as he tried to catch up.

"Ha! You've got to exercise more Lucas! Get your butt out of your dorm room and go on the adventure with me, will ya?" Josh laughed and asked.

Lucas grunted in frustration then yelled back while laughing, "Don't you think that I can't get you! You're doomed!" Then he ran after Josh.

Ares slowly walked and observed them from behind. He tried to skip like Josh, but instead, he stepped onto his shoelaces and landed on his face.

Classes finished at three, and the boys headed towards the office for detention. They walked into the administrative building while Lucas almost forced Josh not to skip or do anything silly. Lucas and Ares left when they reached the dean's office.

Josh twisted the door handle and opened it slowly. He was relieved to find that he was not alone. Then, after looking at the student inside more carefully, he was no longer sure if it was a lucky thing to have this companion during detention or not.

It's not that his detention buddy is a polar bear that would munch Josh's fingers for snacks, nor is he a pretentious hypocrite ready to lecture Josh for the rest of the afternoon. Instead, on his foxlike face, there was a slender and sharp nose, long curly black hair that spread behind his head, thin and pale mouth, and the lurking black eyes of a weary falcon. One may be fooled by the thin layer of lazy fog floating across the boy's eyes, yet it was obvious that it would require little effort for him to cut through the fog and strike directly at your eyes. The only color in his outfit was a drooping sunflower pinned on his shirt. Facing the door as if he was welcoming Josh, the boy sat on a black wooden chair behind a table with his legs crossed, holding a book in his hand. He seemed more like a young supervisor than a student.

"Hi, what are you reading?" Josh asked, trying to break the silence.

"Oh, it's *The Prince* by Machiavelli. Just a normal casual history book," Machiavelli spoke calmly. He pulled out a chair next to him and gave Josh a gentle smile. Josh pushed his head down and walked towards him.

"You're a freshman?" Machiavelli asked, actively turning his body towards Josh as he took a seat.

Josh smiled and nodded. His instinct was telling him that there was danger lurking in the corner, yet he reassured himself about how he shouldn't be nervous. It is just him and a friendly upperclassman serving detention.

"Nothing to worry about," he thought.

"I am a senior. My name is Machiavelli Maestro. Nice to meet you." He reached out his hand, giving Josh a calm handshake. Just then, a cold wind slashed through the window into the room. Josh shivered.

"Is it too cold outside? I'll go close the window for you." Machiavelli stood up and stepped in front of the window. Josh could then see his hands. His pumped veins were scattered on the back of his pale hands like scars from eagle's claws. He slowly slid the window shut.

"So, my friend, why are you here?" Machiavelli asked while pulling out a silver dagger from his pocket. He held the handle gently, twirling it like an orchestra conductor.

"I was, um, being stupid and overly expressive in the dining hall," said Josh. He looked down and clasped his hands together.

"Specifically?" Machiavelli further probed

"Jumping onto a chair." Josh said. He looked down with his cheeks burning.

"Haha, don't worry, I'm not more mature than you," Machiavelli laughed. "It indicates the abundance of your energy and happiness. In fact, your fresh energy is exactly what we, dull and unfeeling upperclassmen, need," he said while handing the little dagger to Josh.

"You're not stuffy, in fact, you are very, um, interesting!" Josh said, trying to come up with something cheerful because he cannot think of a perfect word to describe him. He was very friendly, yet Josh uncontrollably shivered in his presence. Then, Josh took the dagger with both hands, and he saw a line of words carved into the blade and painted red: *Principes Non Homines.*

"Thanks, and that's why I'm here. I am too "interesting" for the dean to not give me detention," he said. Pointing at the phrase on the body of the blade, he commanded, "take a guess at what it means."

"Ha, apparently the word 'fun' is not in the dean's dictionary," Josh laughed, then, looking at the carvings, he asked, "Principles are not human?"

"You are close," Machiavelli replied appreciatively, "It reminds me to be a leader, not an ordinary man. You don't feel like a person who would transform into an ordinary boring upperclassman in the future. You feel like a future leader, Josh." he smiled as he praised Josh.

Blushing, Josh is a little unbalanced by this unexpected appreciation; he said while holding onto the edge of his chair, "Thank you-!"

"I know a place where there are many *Principes* like you. I am their leader, and we would do a lot of fun things together," he said, cutting Josh off. Taking a glance at Josh's shoes, which were covered in mud and grass, he continued, "we hike, visit abandoned haunted houses, camp, and go on a lot of different adventures."

He stood up with his falcon-like body slightly leaning towards Josh, saying, "Josh, imagine escaping the dean's and your teacher's expectation and rules; imagine seeking freedom with interesting people," his falcon eyes pierced deep inside Josh's eyes this time. He commanded, "imagine going on a truly epic adventure with your true friends."

He leaped towards the door. Josh tried to stand up and give him the dagger, but he just squeezed out a word or two.

"Machiavelli, your dagger," he called out.

"Don't worry. Bring it back to me tomorrow. Meet me in the dressing room in the school theater. I'll show you around." Machiavelli turned and said in a calm voice. He then opened the door and left the office.

Josh was left on the chair, stunned and with fire burning inside him.

He picked up the dagger again, staring closely into the word "*Principes*" carved onto the blade, overlooking how the red paint glinted under the light.

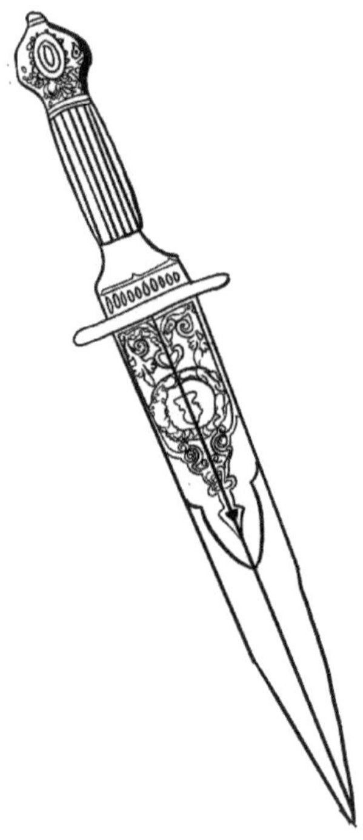

"Okay, let me make this clear," said Lucas. "A weird, stranger upperclassmen gave you contraband and told you to meet him in the abandoned dressing room, and you want to take us with you?" He queried, laughing, and frowning. The three boys sat on their dorm's common room sofa. It was a cheap green sofa with holes and stains all over the place. You wouldn't be surprised to find a bag of leftover chips or a pack of expired cigarettes in the creases.

Josh replied, "Look! This super cool guy, called Machiavelli or something like that, said that he has this amazing club where you guys get to go on adventures and have a lot of fun!" Ares was squeezed between Lucas and Josh, becoming the buffer zone for their debate.

Sly Josh realized that Ares never really said "no" to any of his proposals, so he asked, "Hey Ares! Joining the club is a fantastic idea, right?"

Ares looked at Josh and Lucas hesitantly, then he stood up and said, "Sorry guys I have some work to do, I'll catch up with you later!" He scuttled back to his dorm.

"Hey, how about this?" Josh tried to bargain, "How about we forget about the whole adventure thing, and let's join this club instead!"

Lucas rolled his eyes and walked back to his room.

"I'll take that as a yes!" Josh yelled. He stared at Lucas' back for a moment, then followed him back to the dorm area.

Josh couldn't focus adjusting the water temperature when he was showering, he couldn't look at what's in front of him when he's walking, and he couldn't think of cells or organelles when doing his biology homework. He couldn't hold onto his pencil anymore, so he shoved it back into its case and pulled out the dagger from his table drawer. Lustrous, golden, and heavy, just like the adventures he thinks he's going on; Josh couldn't take his hands off it.

Josh took the boys backstage to the dressing room the very next day, after class. It was a five-minute walk from their dorms to the theater, and the boys, all excited to varying degrees, chatted along the way.

Walking behind the two, Ares called Josh and Lucas, waving at them. "Hey, will you slow down just a bit?" He asked.

Josh and Lucas were engaged in a fierce debate about whether there is a ghost in the dressing room or not. "I promise! The school put on *Macbeth* three years ago, and the lead actor playing Macbeth tried to kill himseer4tlf with the prop dagger after the final show!" Josh yelled.

"Shush! Who even told you that?" Lucas questioned doubtfully.

"My prefect! He's a Senior, and he was telling us ghost stories yesterday." Josh claimed confidently.

"Oh boy! Firstly, my brother was in that play when he was a senior, and he did not tell me anything about students killing each other and stuff," Lucas refuted. "If someone died, it would have been on the news three years ago. Do you remember seeing something like a 'high school student found dead in a theater' on the daily news? Not to mention how ghost stories are not credible at all. Really, read less murder mysteries, oh wait, I forgot, you don't really read at all…"

The debate quickly escalated into an all-out argument. "Okay, shut up Lucas, this is real!" "You shut up!" "Stop yelling!" …..

"Hey!!" Ares' voice put an end to the argument. "We're here."

They opened the door and found that no lights were on inside the auditorium. They turned on their cell phone camera's flashlight, then closed the door. Along with the echoing of the slammed door in the darkness, they tiptoed on to the stage, went backstage, and then carefully crossed the cordon separating the old dressing room from the rest of the building. Josh knocked on the slightly moldy wooden door. A few seconds later, possibly after some whispering inside the room, a person walking in calm, patterned footsteps came to open the door.

"Hi, Josh. I see you brought your friends with you. Don't worry, the more members we have the better our adventures will be. Welcome to the base of the Icarus club." Machiavelli warmly greeted Josh. He then gestured for the three boys to join him inside the dressing room. The only sources of light in the dark room were a few candles placed around different dressing tables and one set of makeup lights that glitched periodically. There were around ten upperclassmen scattered around the room, welcoming the three new members with a mixture of curiosity and contempt.

"Hey, this is the boy I told you about earlier today, he brought his friends with him." Machiavelli said to the girl who was sitting in the middle of the room. The very fit girl with broad shoulders had her fiery ginger hair tied up into a ponytail, probably so that she could weight-lift and do cross-country more conveniently.

"All right, Mac'n Cheese, let me talk to them." The girl spoke loudly. Machiavelli sighed and then walked to one of the corners of the room. Feeling some weird tension and pressure, the boys straightened their backs, standing upright like new recruits entering boot camp when the girl marched towards them.

The girl spoke as if she were commanding, "Alright, kids, I'm Victoria, a senior, and the leader of the Icarus Club. Now tell me your names!"

"I'm Josh! Nice meeting you!"

"I, I, um, I'm Ares."

"My name is Lucas King."

The girl suddenly lit up on hearing Lucas' name. "Oh, so you are Andrew King's brother! He was a senior during my freshman year, we were in the same theater ensemble!"

You could hear the overflowing joy in Victoria's voice. She went up and shook Lucas' hand very powerfully, leaving Lucas flattered. Machiavelli sighed again.

"Hey, Mac'n Cheese, why so sad? Anyways, if Andrew's brother is in the crew, I'll be very happy to take them and do the initiation next weekend." Victoria confidently said. Her voice, annunciation, and gestures demonstrated a pure presence. The other members nodded at her words.

"Wait, what's the initiation about?" questioned Lucas.

One of the members said, "If you want to join our club, you've got to prove that you're capable of completing adventures with us! You've got to do something to prove your strength! Hey boss, what are those rookies doing this year? What about running naked around the campus? Ha!" He laughed and mocked the three boys.

Just before Victoria tried to share her ideas, Machiavelli interrupted and proposed for them to take their tests at the cliff. His proposal received devious smiles and giggles from his audience.

Victoria hushed the crowd and spoke to the boys, "Okay, any questions before I let you go?"

Josh raised his hand and asked, "Why are we located in the abandoned dressing room?"

"We're not really an actual club," Victoria said, "cause no teachers would approve students going out there and doing crazy stuff and things like that. So, we weren't given any official meeting place a few years ago. Thanks to Machiavelli, who has some connections with the theater director, we get to use this old dressing room for meetings! Machiavelli's a pretty good actor. Hey, Mac'n Cheese, what's the first show you were in?" Victoria asked. She then recalled and laughed, "Macbeth in freshman year"? Oh yeah! I was on the running team back then. They wanted me in the team because I was good at lifting stuff, ha!"

While everyone laughed, Lucas spotted Machiavelli glancing in his direction with a dangerous, threatening gleam in his eyes. When he tried to take a better look, he had already switched back into the calm, elegant senior.

Th boys said goodbye to the seniors and club members and proceeded out of the door, with Josh and Lucas discussing some topics, and Machiavelli's hawk-like vision spotted Ares, walking behind them with his head down.

Next week, Victoria took the boys and Machiavelli to the cliff behind the school. They snuck out of school by crossing the forest and then climbing over a wall strewn with barbed wire.

"Is she sure about what she is doing?" Lucas asked concernedly.

"Shush! You don't want to be the misfit, right?" whispered Ares as they marched up the hill to the cliff.

"All right boys! We're here!" Victoria yelled at the group while she pointed down at the lake beneath them.   Josh looked down at the cliff.

 "Boys, this is the sacred initiation! Machiavelli, mind explaining it?" She asked. He nodded and smiled, then calmly said, "It is very straightforward, just jump." Lucas and Ares gasped and took a step back.

"Whoa, Mr. Bad Guy, don't frighten these freshmen?" Viktoria laughed. She then looked at all three of the boys with a much more serious look, and said, "This is a very important tradition that we have performed and passed down since the first club meeting fifty years ago. This is not just a silly act, boys; this jump holds a legacy. By jumping, you will be proving yourself true fighter." She patted Ares' shoulder and said, "you can quit now and regret it for the rest of your life, or go for it and jump, boys! Do it! Do it for the part inside of you thirsty for adventure."

Lub-dub, lub-dub, lub-dub, lub-dub..." Josh heard his heart pounding. He saw the dagger. Blood rushed into his muscles, leaving his hands and feet pale and cold. His heart was pounding so hard he believed that it would break a hole in his chest. Josh had not experienced this weird combination of feelings before blood ran from his head down to his toes, burning ears and aching head.

"Principes, non homines!" Josh charged down the cliff and leapt into the water.

Lub-dub. Water soaked his clothes and filled his ears, nose, and eyes, completely freezing him. Josh felt like being trapped in a huge watery dungeon. The dagger slowly fades backwards.

Lub-dub. Victoria and Lucas rushed to the cliff edge, looking down and frowning. Victoria seemed calm, but Lucas had completely forgotten his etiquette and manners. His face was pale when he screamed down into the lake desperately: "You moron! JOSH! YOU MORON!"

Lub-dub. Josh struggled to open his eyes under the water. The rush of blood forced him to stay awake, swim upwards, and swim toward the dagger.

Lub-dub. Collapsed onto the ground, Ares stared into the dirt while Machiavelli stood next to him, overlooking the water.

Splash! Josh's head emerged from the water like a triumphant gladiator, and he waved cheerfully at the crowd looking down at him. He saw Victoria clapping very proudly and Lucas jumping up and down and swinging his jacket like a maniacal cowboy. Machiavelli, who was shocked, surprised, and hardly noticeably annoyed, applauded in Josh's direction.

"The East Coast sun has never been so bright," Josh thought happily.

The Icarus Club has become a significant part of Josh's life, never missing any club meetings on Tuesdays or weekend trips to the cliff except that one meeting where Josh had to make up for an exam. While Ares became much more busy with his emails somehow and showed up to every single event, Lucas only went with Josh on some Tuesdays.

After school, Josh went to a club meeting with Lucas. Usually, Victoria would bring snacks and a small projector, and they would play horror movies to "harden member's courage." Today, there were no candies, no movies, and no Victoria. Standing elegantly next to the door, Machiavelli told us that Victoria would be back soon.

He repeated his words for several days until the day when alternating red and blue lights and the wail of police sirens intruded the calm campus. Officers in dark blue uniforms holding notebooks and making phone calls took students out of their classrooms to collect evidence. During biology, two officers came in and whispered some words to the teacher.

"Lucas, please go with these gentlemen, they'll need to ask you some questions." The teacher said. Lucas stood up, pushed his chair inside the table with his trembling hands, and followed the officers out of the classroom. Later that night in the common room, Lucas brought back terrible news with him.

"Josh, Ares, Victoria is dead." Lucas's cry was met with absolute silence. He collapsed onto the sofa and covered his face with a pillow and shivered.

Ares came up to him, patted him on the shoulders, then ran back to his dorm. Josh stared in the direction in which Ares left, then sat next to Lucas.

"What happened?" he asked as he wiped and rubbed his sweaty palms on the sofa pillow. His clothes were soaked and sticky.

Lucas shivered while recalling as much information as possible, "The police found Victoria's body downstream, where water plants tangled her ankle and prevented her from floating further downriver. Their initial theory is that she suicided by drowning herself in the river." Josh had never seen Lucas panicking before.

Josh knew that he should say something nice or at least give Lucas a pat on the shoulder, but fear pushed him to keep on asking, "Lucas, was there anything weird that happened recently?"

Lucas' emotional burden did not stop him from thinking. He wiped off the sweat on his face with the sleeves of the jacket he was wearing and responded, "Yes, Josh, yes. Something felt off at the meeting a few weeks ago that you didn't attend...

People were celebrating the end of first quarter at the meeting which Josh missed. Lucas decided to go to the mini party solely for the deserts. He asked Ares whether he wanted to come along.

"Will Machiavelli, um, and Victoria, yes, and Victoria be there?" Ares asked.

"Of course, it's their club after all," replied Lucas, slightly confused.

When they entered the dressing room, the members had decorated the entire room with red and blue LED lights. Victoria, who was surprisingly wearing an orange dress, was passing out chocolate cookies she brought, while Machiavelli filled red plastic cups with a cocktail made of lime soda and cheap smuggled whiskey.

"It's nice to have some connections, and don't tell your brother, Andrew, that I'm allowing you to drink," Machiavelli joked as he gave Lucas and Ares each a red cup filled with beverages, and he added, "No seconds allowed; I don't want you guys to get drunk, get caught, and get everyone here into trouble. "

After getting cookies, the two sat on one of the dressing desks in the corner. Lucas took a sip of the cocktail, frowned, and forced himself to swallow it down. He took out his napkin and wiped the beads of sweat off on his forehead.

"Tastes worst then the dining hall dispenser's greyish grape juice." He complained to Ares. "It's weird that I'm asking you this question, but how have you been doing lately?"

"I mean, it's not terrible. You remember that one time where you and Josh were skipping, and then I tried to skip as well, but fell instead? I'd say that I'm gradually learning how to skip right now." Ares replied, laughing kind of bitterly.

Lucas paused for a second. He knew that he and Josh weren't treating Ares the best way. Apologies and words came to his mind, but instead he grabbed two more pieces of cookies and gave one to Ares. They sat there, eating cookies and sipping on alcohol with both of their heads down.

A few minutes later, Ares stood up and said, "Thank you for coming here with me." He then gently walked towards the door of the noisy party room.

"Hey Ares, see you soon!" yelled out Lucas.

With his back towards Lucas, Ares paused, then waved back. "See you soon," he said as he walked out of the room.

Watching Ares' back, Lucas took a larger sip and frowned. He then looked into the partying crowd to distract himself. Some boys were doing silly dances, a girl was scribbling stars on her shoe, and Machiavelli was at the same dressing desk with Victoria. Slightly blushing, most likely due to the cocktail, Victoria took big gulps of the liquid while Machiavelli sat next to her, smiling, then sighing. Victoria leaned towards Machiavelli, whispered into his ears, then backed out and laughed at him, who's face has turned red. However, again, Lucas saw that for a split-second, Machiavelli showed off the same fearsome gleam, forcing Lucas to hide under one of the tables.

Lucas also saw something else that Victoria did not. When everyone else has left, Machiavelli turned his back to Victoria, added something into the cup, then filled the cup with cocktail and gave it to Victoria.

"You like my dress?"

"Um, I suppose..."

"Mac'n Cheese, my good sir, your face is burning, ha!"

"Come on, Vic, Want some more drink?"

"Promise me," Victoria said as she took the drink from Machiavelli, placed it next to her, and held out her pinkie finger. She whispered again. Machiavelli held out his slightly trembling little finger, nodded, and made a pinkie swear with some beads of tear dangling in his eyes. Afraid that Machiavelli would notice him, Lucas snuck out of the room.

Lucas did not see how they then both took a big gulp of their drinks and locked eyes. They stood up as Victoria leaned closer and closer to Machiavelli, eventually till there was only a couple of centimeters between Victoria's round nose and Machiavelli's sharp nose. She grabbed his collar with her right hand and reached for Machiavelli's face with the other, gently leaving it on his burning cheek. She noticed Machiavelli's watery eyes, and he noticed the moist gathering on her cheek. She laughed, pulled him even closer towards her, closed her eyes, and right before their lips touched each other, she collapsed into Machiavelli's arms and slowly slid down to the floor.

Machiavelli covered his face with his hands, kneeled next to lifeless Victoria, and wept quietly yet uncontrollably. His tears slid down his face and fell onto her ginger hair and her back.

"I'm sorry, I, I, really, this terrible, this…," said a man who stood outside the room.

"*Whack*". Machiavelli slapped himself in the face brutally and said, "This is for my plan. Let's get this over with…"

Josh and Lucas felt alone and powerless. They had promised to investigate what happened that night, but all efforts so far proved fruitless. Few things were there to be searched online, and the police officers hadn't made any announcements yet. Ares, on the other hand, rarely spoke to them after Victoria's death. Whenever Josh or Lucas wanted to wave hello to him, he would immediately run away in the opposite direction. Even if the two knocked on Ares' door, they got no response, except the tireless typing noise originating from his room which he had told them he was emailing Machiavelli. Weeks of searching and investigating made the two tired. After soaking themselves in the library for another two hours, Lucas decided to go back to his dorm.

"I'm too tired for this," he yawned.

Josh stretched his arms and responded; "Sure, I'll talk to you later if I get anything useful.

"See you!"

"Goodnight Lucas!"

After going through and trying almost every topic, Josh did not know what else to search.

"Wait! The ghost story about senior student suiciding, might as well search that one. "Josh thought, hoping that he could draw some connections between the two deaths across the span of three years.

After typing in the key words, an article popped out.

" *Special Student Interviews with Andrew King & Marvel Maestro: Shakespeare Festival and* Macbeth, this doesn't seem right," Josh thought as he closed the computer screen.

"Plip-plop, plip-plop …" A couple of small rain drops periodically landed on the roof. Josh sat in front of the computer screen inside his dorm, staring into its blinding lights and allowing his arms to hang over the edge of his table. The screen replays the news video, where the woman sitting behind the screen squeaked, "There has been two deaths in the past month at a local high school. Victoria Webster, 18-year-old, was found in the river near the school three weeks ago. Reports from the medical examiners proves the cause of death is food poisoning." Josh recalls her hair and the way she cheered when he jumped off the cliff.

The woman continued, "Lucas King, 15-years-old, has been severely injured by his classmate, Ares Zhu. He suffered serious injuries and attempts to resuscitate him were unsuccessful. It must be noticed that Zhu has turned himself in right after stabbing Lucas in seventeen different locations with a dagger...”

“Plip-plop, plip-plop, plipplop plipop ...” The rain drops hit the roof more rapidly.

Then they started clattering against the windows panes, drumming the walls, pounding the wooden floor, and suddenly, SPLASH! It started to rain, as if someone up in the clouds poured a bucket of water down on us; there was water everywhere.

It was obvious that his school was not prepared for such heavy rain. Water overflowed the sewage and flooded, as if the water was thrusting past itself to get ahead. Heavy raindrops fell on the feeble flowers and grass on the sidewalk like bombs from a bomber, blasted like machine gun fire at the flowers until they bent and kneeled.

Josh stood up and opened his door. He wanted to run. Facing the rain head on, he dashed out of his dorm, down the hill as if he was racing the flooding water. His jacket and sweater quickly became soaked, and the rain stuck his wet, cold clothes to his body. Though it felt like needles were piercing his skin, he kept on running.

Josh ran into the forest, where the rain penetrated the ceiling of leaves and smashed his face and drove into his eyes. He stepped on leaves and slipped, landing on his back. Sticky muddy water was pushed into his sweater; he felt a stimulating and chilling pain. He kept on running.

The raindrops hit his glasses, and his skin felt the collision of the rain splashing it, just like how he had run straight into that huge, gigantic wall when he saw Lucas carried away in the ambulance and Ares taken by the police. Blood on his forehead, tears dangling in those once, pure black eyes, he kept on running.

He stopped when he reached the soccer field across the forest and down the hill; the same where he, Ares, Luca, and Machiavelli once played soccer together. Machiavelli was a brilliant goalkeeper, and Josh never scored a goal when Machiavelli was defending. When they were together, the skies always shined brightly. He lifted his head and reached for his blurry glasses which were covered with muddy water. He tried to clean them by scrubbing them with his jacket. The wet cloth only made them blurrier. He then turned to his right and saw the empty goal. Lucas was not there to help him, but Machiavelli was not there to defend it. He ran into one of the nets to grab a deflated and soaked soccer ball and he pushed it onto the penalty spot.

"One time," he whispered. He then backed away for a few steps, staring at the soccer ball. He leaned forward and sprinted.

Yelling furiously as he sprinted toward the ball:

"Ahhhhhhhh!" His war-cry could have scraped a hole in the sky.

"Cling." Thats the sound of the ball hitting the goal post.

"Why? Why? WHY?" Josh cried furiously and he ran toward the goal post, punching and kicking it like a barbarian.

"Do you have to take everything from me, everything?" The rain was still smacking, and the sharp sound of rain hitting hard metal was like mocking giggles. Josh collapsed and lay down on the grass inside the net. All that he saw was dark clouds, grey skies, and the net resembling iron bars. There were no more bright blue skies left.   He felt frustrated for not investigating enough; he was disappointed for not protecting his friends; he felt weirdly lonely because all his friends except Machiavelli had left him; he also felt guilty for bring his friends to the club since everything went straight downhill after joining Icarus and meeting

Machiavelli.

"Wait! Machiavelli!" Josh suddenly burst up. The ghost stories about students suiciding during the school play *Macbeth*, Lucas and his brother, Ares constantly emailing Machiavelli and avoiding the two, Victoria and Machiavelli's promises, and the prop dagger all suddenly came clearly to Josh's mind.

Hearing footsteps, Josh suddenly turned around.

"Is that a dagger that I see before me?"

"Too late, Josh."

June 26th, 2021

Today is supposed to be a happy day. If Andrew didn't kill my brother with the dagger. I lost my brother today.

June 27th, 2021

I couldn't write yesterday because the police took me for questions immediately after the show and I'm way too tired to do so. I have prepared a surprise for my brother, the star of the show playing Macbeth himself! So, I hid under the dressing desk in our changing room with my present so I could surprise him. Instead, when Andrew King, one of the other seniors, was playing with the prop dagger, my brother ran into the dagger deliberately. Red, sticky liquid covered the floor, and some reached the place under the table. My shoes and presents were covered with my brother's blood.

June 30th, 2021

I do not care that he died because he ran into the dagger himself, I do not care that he already has several mental issues and it might have been what he wanted to do, and I do not care that Andrew King was merely holding the dagger. Andrew took my brother from me, so he needs to experience the same, insufferable pain. He told me that he had a younger brother, Lucas King, who will be joining high school three years later, when I would become a senior. He would pay.

May 1st, 2022

The dressing room has been abandoned since then, and this girl called Victoria, and I used it as a meeting place for her adventure club thing called Icarus. She was in the play last year, and she was kind despite having terrifying muscles. She is really nice.

June 26th, 2022

It has been one whole year since my brother's death. I have formed the plan to push the kid off the cliff near my school and then let him drown in the river. He needs to pay. Every night, or nearly every night, I dreamed of the dagger, my brother dying in front of me, and Andrew holding the dagger. My pain needs to be shared. Desperately.

August 27th, 2024

It was worth it for me to get this Josh kid into Vic's club, Icarus club. He brought two kids with him, one of them is Lucas King, my target, and the other one, called Ares, could be used as an important tool to complete my plan. I also proposed for Vic to take the kids to the cliff to do the initiation, so that either Lucas would get drowned or someone else, to proves that this method will not work or not.

August 31th, 2024

Vic took the kids to the cliff today. That crazy kid Josh jumped right into the river, and he managed to survive. I do need to think of a new plan. Maybe I could use Ares a bit. He doesn't get enough attention from his two "friends", always walking behind them – but this can make him great for me to exploit a little.

September 15ᵗʰ, 2024

I really don't like what's happening. Vic came up to me today and asked me to not do anything bad with Lucas King. I have completely forgotten that she was also in the play, and was one of the few people who knew what happened that night. If Lucas were dead, she would suspect me and report me... Every time Andrew, the dagger, and my brother hunted me in my dreams, she always listened to me sharing my vulnerability. She seems tough, she never joked or mocked about it when I was sharing. She just listened and called me Mac'n Cheese.

September 16ᵗʰ, 2024

The email manipulation with Ares is going well. I have sort of separated him socially with his other friends. Whenever I do morally incorrect things, Vic with her ginger hair appears in my mind, trying to stop me. Each insult and word I type hurts, but it is all for my brother.

September 18ᵗʰ, 2024

I really don't want to write today. For the plan, Vic must go. I snuck something in her drink that made her pass out, and I had Ares carry her body and leave her in the river. She was stunning in her orange dress, matches very well with her hair. We made a pinkie swear that I won't go after Lucas, and maybe because of the alcohol, she leaned in, where my heart felt her heartbeat. Then she collapsed, right in front of me. I really wish I could hear someone call me Mac'n Cheese, one more time. I'm sorry, Vic. I'm sorry I'm sorry I'm sorry I'm sorry I'm sorry I'm sorry I'm sorry I'm sorry I'm sorry I'm sorry...

October 15ᵗʰ, 2024

Ares completed his job. I gave him my dagger, and now Lucas is in the hospital, and he turned himself in. Brother, can you see me? I'm sorry.

<h1 style="text-align:center">June 26th, 2025</h1>

It has been four years. I lived in guilt, regret, and relief for my brother's vengeance. It has all been settled.

Or has it? To be candid I did not hate the entire process. Actually, I valued the slow, torturing process in which manipulation emails were sent, rather than gaining revenge. I love Victoria. It's not about her kindness, her dress, or her hair. I loved how her emerald eyes shook when she collapsed into my arms. I loved how she let out her last breath. It was sweet with a light scent of lime cocktail. I loved how calm, lifeless Victoria in her orange dress gently flowed down the river in serenity. Her hair soaked in river water reflected the moonlight. I loved how Victoria and I built this wonderful relationship: doing plays, building a club together, and going through adventures, just so that I could kill her and sabotage everything we created. Now that her physical body is gone, she can stand by me in my memories forever.

I really miss her, and I feel the urge to build the next relationship for me to destroy. Who will be next....

CONCLUSION

These two short stories were selected from others already written and yet more never put to paper – I do sincerely hope you enjoyed them and look forward to regaling you in the future to sequels and prequels.